A Note to Parents

Your child is beginning the lifelong adventure of reading! And with the **World of Reading** program, you can be sure that he or she is receiving the encouragement needed to become a confident, independent reader. This program is specially designed to encourage your child to enjoy reading at every level by combining exciting, easy-to-read stories featuring favorite characters with colorful art that brings the magic to life.

The **World of Reading** program is divided into four levels so that children at any stage can enjoy a successful reading experience:

Reader-in-Training
Pre-K–Kindergarten

Picture reading and word repetition for children who are getting ready to read.

Beginner Reader
Pre-K–Grade 1

Simple stories and easy-to-sound-out words for children who are just learning to read.

Junior Reader
Kindergarten–Grade 2

Slightly longer stories and more varied sentences perfect for children who are reading with the help of a parent.

Super Reader
Grade 1–Grade 3

Encourages independent reading with rich story lines and wide vocabulary that's right for children who are reading on their own.

Learning to read is a once-in-a-lifetime adventure, and with **World of Reading**, the journey is just beginning!

Printed in the United States of America
First Edition
10 9 8 7 6 5 4 3 2 1
G658-7729-4-12245
Library of Congress Control Number: 2012934135

ISBN 978-1-4231-4909-5

For more Disney Press fun, visit www.disneybooks.com
Visit DisneyChannel.com

World of Reading

LEVEL 3

Attack of the Ferb Snatchers!

Adapted by Kristen Depken

Based on the series created by Dan Povenmire & Jeff "Swampy" Marsh

DISNEY PRESS
New York

Late one night, Phineas and Ferb were watching alien movies. Their sister, Candace, decided to watch, too.

"Get me up to speed," she said.

"The aliens are replacing the heads of all the humans with their own heads," Phineas explained. He said that aliens could disguise themselves as humans.

"Then how can you tell they're aliens?" Candace asked.

"There are three classic ways to spot an alien," said Phineas.

Aliens used strange words.

Aliens had weird body parts.

"But the clearest sign," said Phineas, "is that they can safely remove any human head and replace it with their own multi-eyed head."

The alien movie played all night.
Candace stayed awake to watch.

In the end, no one thought the
woman in the movie had really seen
aliens. "Why did I think anyone would
believe me?" she cried. "I was a fool!"

"Oh, my gosh, you guys. That was awesome!" Candace exclaimed. She looked around. "Guys?"

Phineas and Ferb were gone.

Candace ran to find her brothers. On the way, she bumped into her mom, who was carrying a basket of laundry.

The basket fell on the floor.

"Can you take this upstairs?" her mom asked.

Candace held up one of Ferb's shirts.
It was very small.

"How cute." Candace smiled. "Ferb's
torso is so tiny."

Candace found Ferb upstairs in the office. He was talking to someone on the computer.

But the words Ferb used sounded very...strange.

Candace quickly left. She didn't see Ferb take a big piece of chewy candy out of his mouth.

Ferb hadn't been talking at all. The voice Candace had heard was actually Ferb's cousin. He had a Scottish accent.

"Tell Uncle Angus thanks for the candy," Ferb said to his cousin.

Later on, Ferb went to the backyard.
He began working on a special project
in a tent.

Candace came outside, too. She saw
Ferb's shadow through the tent, and
gasped. It looked like Ferb was taking
off his head!

"Oh, my gosh. Ferb's an alien!"
Candace screamed. Then she ran away.

Candace hid in the basement. "I'm sure there's a good reason Ferb can remove his head," she told herself. "It's not like he had any of the other signs."

Then she remembered that Ferb had a small torso and had spoken in a strange language.

"The aliens got to Ferb!" she cried.

Candace ran to get Phineas. "Ferb is an alien!" she told him.

"My brother's an alien?" Phineas asked. "How cool is that! But I think you might be letting your imagination get the best of you, sis."

Candace decided to get proof! She spied on Ferb and took pictures.

In one picture, Ferb looked like he had lots of arms.

In another, he was pulling strange goo out of an invention.

Finally, Candace saw Ferb wearing glasses with lots of eyes. She was sure he was an alien!

Meanwhile, Phineas and Ferb's pet platypus, Perry, was on a mission. The brothers didn't know that Perry was actually a spy named Agent P.

The platypus needed to stop his enemy, Dr. Doofenshmirtz, from selling evil inventions on the Internet.

Agent P dressed up like a mad scientist. Then he went to the evil doctor's lab.

"You must be here about the ad," Dr. Doofenshmirtz said.

Agent P's disguise had tricked him!

The doctor took Agent P over to a giant machine. "Behold, the Wrapped Up in a Nice Little Bow-inator!" he said.

Dr. Doofenshmirtz explained how it worked. "Say your nemesis is arriving sooner than expected, and your place is a mess. Tidying up is a snap with a press of this large, red button."

The doctor pushed the button.

The machine zapped a pile of dirty
sheets on Dr. Doofenshmirtz's bed.

The bed shrunk into a tiny box!

Dr. Doofenshmirtz walked over to a treadmill in his lab. "You can also use the machine to hang your clothes on. Just like a treadmill," he said. "So, make me an offer."

Agent P didn't respond.

"Wow, you're a good negotiator," Dr. Doofenshmirtz said. "Okay, half price."

Just then, Agent P pulled off his disguise!

Dr. Doofenshmirtz gasped. "Perry the Platypus!" He grabbed a baseball bat.

Agent P used his tail to whack the tiny box with the bow at his enemy.

The box hit the treadmill's "start"
button.

The treadmill began to move! Dr.
Doofenshmirtz accidentally knocked
over his baseball collection.

Baseballs bounced everywhere! They hit the red button on Dr. Doofenshmirtz's Wrapped Up in a Nice Little Bow-inator.

Soon, everything in the lab was shrinking into tiny boxes.

Back at home, Candace showed
Phineas the pictures she had taken
of Ferb.

"Look at these photos!" she cried.
"Ferb is an alien!"

"And listen to this!" Candace played a cassette tape for Phineas. No sound came out.

"That is an entirely different silence than the Ferb silence we're used to," she said. "Here, I'll play it backwards."

"Listen, Candace," Phineas interrupted. "As cool as it would be for Ferb to be an alien, that's sadly not the case."

Phineas took Candace outside.
Ferb was there, working in his tent.

Phineas told Ferb that Candace
thought he was from outer space.

"I saw Ferb's head ripped off by an
alien monster!" Candace insisted.

"Oh, you must mean this reverse
power unit we're repairing," Phineas
explained.

He pulled back the tent flap.
Inside was a machine that was shaped
like Ferb's head. It wasn't an alien.

"But what about all this evidence?" Candace asked.

"Even though Ferb's not an alien, we are fixing a spacecraft for a friend," Phineas explained.

"Wait, what?" Candace said.

"We just finished, and we're about to launch," Phineas replied.

Candace couldn't believe it. "You guys are so busted!" she cried.

Candace ran to get her mother. She
found her in the kitchen.

"Mom!" Candace exclaimed. She
grabbed her arm. "Come on. I've got
something to show you!"

Candace dragged her mother to
the backyard.

Suddenly, the lawn opened up. A
giant spaceship and launching pad
rose out of the ground.

"Are you seeing this?" Candace
asked her mom.

"Yes," her mother replied.

"I can't believe this is really happening!" Candace said to her brothers. "I busted you!"

But Candace's mom didn't yell at Phineas and Ferb. She just smiled. "You two have done a great job repairing my ship," she said.

"Huh?" asked Candace.

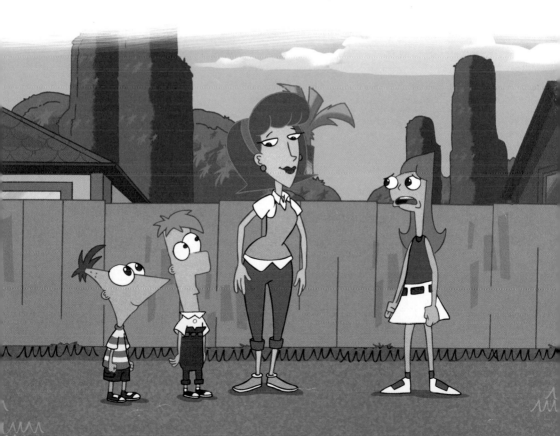

It turned out that the "mom" in the yard was really a robot. Inside was a little alien!

"No problem, Garr-bagg!" Phineas said. The brothers had fixed the alien's broken spaceship.

Candace watched as the little alien
flew past her . . .

. . . and up into its spaceship!

Candace was shocked. There actually had been an alien. And her brothers had gotten away with helping it!

Just then, their real mom's car pulled into the driveway.

The alien ship and robot mom were gone, but the launchpad was still in the backyard.

"I have proof!" cried Candace. She ran to get her real mom.

Back at Dr. Doofenshmirtz's lab,
Agent P hit one of the tiny boxes at his
enemy.

The doctor accidentally swallowed it.
His stomach began to rumble.

The furniture in the box expanded inside Dr. Doofenshmirtz's stomach! When the furniture was back to its normal size, the doctor was huge.

"Why did I ever order such a large bedroom set?" he moaned.

Suddenly, the Wrapped Up in a Nice Little Bow-inator rolled out the window. Agent P didn't have any time to lose!

He jumped onto the machine and pressed the button. Dr. Doofenshmirtz's whole lab shrunk into a tiny box with a bow.

Agent P flew away on a parachute.

Before it hit the ground, the machine shot one last laser beam up into the air. It bounced off a satellite . . .

. . . and right into Phineas and Ferb's backyard! The alien launchpad shrunk into a tiny box.

"It folds up for easy storage," said Phineas. "Cool."

A moment later, Candace brought her mom into the backyard. By that point, the launchpad was gone.

"No!" cried Candace. "But it was all right here."

Candace dropped to her knees.
"Oh, why did I think anyone
would believe me?" she cried. "I was
a fool! A fool!"

Candace's life suddenly seemed a
lot like a movie.